CHILD OF THE SUN

To Monica, my half-Cuban, blonde-haired, green-eyed child
with sparkling eyes and the lovely smile.   —S.M.A.

This edition published in 2003.

Copyright © 1995 by Troll Communications L.L.C.

Printed in Canada

10   9   8   7   6   5   4   3

Library of Congress Cataloging-in-Publication Data

Arnold, Sandra Martin.
Child of the sun: a Cuban legend / retold by Sandra Arnold;
illustrated by Dave Albers.
p. cm.—(Legends of the world)
Summary: Greedy Sun refuses to share the sky with Moon in this
Cuban legend that explains why solar eclipses occur.
ISBN 0-8167-3747-9 (lib.)   ISBN 0-8167-3748-7 (pbk.)
[1. Folklore—Cuba.   2. Solar eclipses—Folklore.]   I. Albers, Dave,
ill.   II. Title.   III. Series.
PZ8. 1.A7297Ch   1995   398.2'097291'06—dc20   95-13230

CHILD OF THE SUN

A CUBAN LEGEND

RETOLD BY SANDRA ARNOLD   ILLUSTRATED BY DAVE ALBERS

TROLL ASSOCIATES

Long ago, Earth lived in harmony with her children, Sun and Moon. So she decreed that Sun would rule the day, his warmth and light coaxing the land to grow more plants. At the end of each day, he would leave the sky. Then Moon would watch over the night, ruling the oceans and the seas.

Sun and Moon both promised to abide by her decree, so Earth closed her eyes and fell into a deep slumber.

5

Before long, Sun grew bored and restless with no one to admire him. Reaching down one golden ray, he gathered fine sand from the shores of the bay, rich clay from the valleys, and shimmering copper from the mountains. He mixed them, molded and shaped them, until he created a figure that pleased him.

Whirling around, his rays spinning faster and faster, Sun sang, "Takare', chin, chin, chin. Takare', dundu'. Abri mensu, dun, dun!" As he danced around the figure, he blew the breath of life into its nostrils.

The figure shivered at Sun's caress, then slowly opened his eyes. Seeing his father blazing before him, the first man stood and bowed low.

"Kio, kio, Father Sun," he said. "I am your willing servant."

Sun named this first man Hamao.

Hamao soon made friends with the other creatures of Earth. From them he learned how to find food and shelter. But as the days passed, he grew sad and lonely.

One night Moon heard Hamao crying.

"Hamao, why do you weep?" she asked. "You are lord of all that surrounds you. The trees bend their branches to give you ripe fruit, the animals come to your call, and the flowers caress you with sweet-smelling petals."

"That is true," Hamao said. "But there is no one with whom to share my life. All my animal friends have families, but I have no one to care about me, no one to share whispers in the night. Each day I greet Sun, but he cares nothing about me."

Gentle Moon took pity on Hamao. From her large clay jar, she poured a tiny trickle of celestial dew. Softly, she blew across the small puddle. A cloud of fog rose, twisting gently in the cool night air.

Hamao sighed in wonder as the cloud took form and grew, slowly becoming a woman.

"Guanaroca," Moon whispered her name, and the first woman opened her eyes.

"Oh, Moon, she is beautiful," Hamao said, reaching out his hand. "Her hair is dark as ebony. Her skin is like mahogany. And her smile is as sweet as orange blossoms."

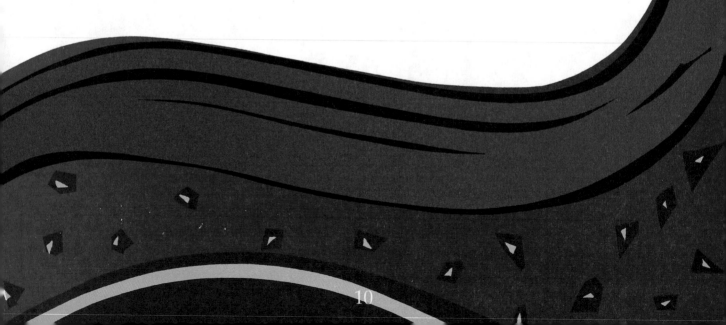

As the seasons brought their changes to Earth, Guanaroca and Hamao grew to love each other. Out of their love a child was born, a son they called Imao.

Moon smiled down at the birth of her grandson. Each night she sent warm breezes to tickle his soft skin and happy dreams to fill his tiny head. But his grandfather, Sun, was angry when he realized he was expected to share Hamao's affection.

"This is all Moon's fault," Sun blazed as his rage grew. "She created the woman who gave birth to this child and stole Hamao away from me."

Sun decided he would find someone else to love only him, but this time he would not create a man. Instead, he would take the child, Imao, and raise him away from his parents and Moon. The child would be Sun's alone.

One hot summer evening Sun crept into the far eastern corner of the sky. As Moon slept, he wrapped her tightly in a web of thick, dark clouds. Now she would interfere with him no more. Moon would sleep forever, and Sun alone would rule the sky.

Then Sun stole into the hut where Hamao and Guanaroca slept. He wrapped Imao in one golden ray and carried him up into the sky.

At the top of a tall mountain, far from all the animals and the birds, Sun gently lay Imao down. Imao woke, cradled against cold stone, and began to cry. He was lonely, hungry, and frightened.

"Hush, hush." Sun stroked the child with warm rays, trying to comfort him. But Imao didn't want the warmth of Sun. He wanted only his mother's embrace, and so he continued to cry.

Far away, in their small hut, Guanaroca heard her baby weeping. She reached over to comfort him, but her hand touched only a coarse woven mat. She sat up, heart pounding, and shook her sleeping husband.

"Hamao! Wake up. Our son is gone!"

Hamao and Guanaroca raced out of the hut. Desperate, they searched the nearby forest but could find no trace of their child.

"My friends," Hamao called out to the animals. "Help me find my son!"

The word was spread far and wide, and all of the animals began to search for Imao.

It was the blue heron, soaring far above Earth, who finally spotted the child on the mountaintop. He swooped down to reach him, but Sun spit tongues of fire and forced him away.

Circling around the mountain, the blue heron waited for Sun to set. Hours passed, and Sun continued to blaze. Finally the heron flew to the hut of Hamao and Guanaroca.

"Sun has taken Imao," he said, "and he will not let me bring him back. Mighty Sun refuses to leave the sky."

"Sun," Guanaroca whispered in horror. How could anyone fight Sun? Surely her child would die.

In a voice filled with pain, Guanaroca cried into the wind, "My child, my child! Someone must help me save my child!"

Wind heard Guanaroca and was touched by her pain. She spread herself across the heavens, searching until she found Moon. Whipping herself into hurricane force, Wind blew away Moon's prison of dark clouds.

Moon woke to the lingering echo of Guanaroca's cry. Looking down, she saw the frightened humans, and Earth withering under the hot sun.

"Follow me," she shouted to Wind. "We must rescue Imao and stop Sun or he will burn Earth to cinders!"

Moon and Wind streaked across the hot sky to the far corner where Sun blazed.

"Return Imao to his parents, Sun, then leave," Moon called to her brother. "Remember your promise to Earth. It is time for night to fall, and the night is mine to rule."

"Never!" Sun shouted. "Night will never fall again. I will no longer share the sky with you. Imao is mine, and I will stay here to make sure no one steals him from me." He whipped a ray of scorching fire at his sister, Moon.

Wind blew the fire away from her friend. And Moon reached down to Earth to fill her clay jar with the cool waters of the ocean and sea. Then she flung the water at Sun.

Sizzling in fury, Sun threw blazing circles of flame at Moon. Moon twisted and dodged as she reached down for more water. Lifting her jar, she doused her brother's shooting flames.

Sun yelled in rage as the air about him filled with white clouds of steam. His anger blazed hotter, and he hurled flashing spears of fire at Moon.

Singed and dirty, Moon twisted away. Again she gathered water to douse her brother's flames, forcing her clay jar deep into the raging ocean.

As the battle flared above, Wind slipped down from the sky. Over the mountains she drifted, until she spotted Imao. She wrapped the child in her strong arms and carried him away.

Sun screamed in fury as he saw the child being taken. His cry tore through the heavens, echoing until it woke Earth.

Earth shook off her dreams and rumbled with anger as she realized her children were fighting. Above her the heavens trembled with bolts of fire and swirling eruptions of steam.

"Sun," she shouted. "Stop this battle! You have broken the promise you made to me."

As soon as his mother spoke, Sun stopped fighting. He looked down at Earth, singed and blackened by stray bolts of fire.

"See what you have done, my child," Earth said.

Sun saw the pain and fear of the animals and humans, the great destruction his pride had caused. He was filled with shame.

Earth gestured to Moon and drew her forward. As she passed in front of Sun, her shadow began to blot out his golden rays. Finally Moon stood in front of her brother, and the long day dimmed to twilight.

Darkness fell on Earth, but it was a strange, shadowy darkness, as if Sun were being eaten by Moon. After the long day, would there now be a long night? Without Sun the plants would die, and there would be no food to eat!

"Earth, bring back Sun," Hamao and Guanaroca cried. "We cannot live without him."

Birds and animals took up the cry, each in its own words, as Sun crept slowly into the west and allowed the night to fall.

Moon took the child, Imao, from the arms of Wind and brought him to his parents.

"Hush. Sleep now," she whispered to Hamao, Guanaroca, and Imao. "Tomorrow all will be as it should." Then she picked up her jar and poured her celestial dew onto Earth, comforting and healing her wounds.

Never again did Sun try to rule the sky alone. From that day forward he was content to share with his sister. But sometimes, even now, when Sun seems restless and bored, Moon will step in front of him and remind him of his promise. When Sun and Moon stand in the sky this way we call it an eclipse.

The Caribbean Islands

Many cultures from around the world have stories to explain natural events. *Child of the Sun* is one such story, which the Ciboney people of Cuba tell to explain the phenomenon of an eclipse. The Ciboney were one of the original inhabitants of Cuba. During prehistoric times, they had traveled from South America across the sea in dugout canoes.

In 1492 the explorer Christopher Columbus landed in Cuba. Claiming the island for Spain, Columbus wrote, "It is the most beautiful land ever seen by human eyes." Indeed, Cuba is a beautiful island with its great plain, rolling hills, and mountains. The Sierra Maestra, a range of steep mountains, is located in the southeastern part of the island. Cuba's coast has so many deep, safe harbors that it has been called "the Isle of a Hundred Harbors."

In 1511 the Spanish began to settle the island, and Cuba soon became one of the richest colonies in the West Indies. Crops, including sugar and tobacco, grew on the large plantations. Native Americans, forced to work in the plantation fields, died of mistreatment and disease. As the Indian population diminished, the Spanish imported African slaves. Today about three-fourths of Cuba's ten million people are of Spanish descent, while the rest are of African or mixed ancestry. Spanish is the official language, and most of the country's traditions and customs are of Spanish origin.